Dear Parent:
Your child's love of reading starts here!

Every child learns to read in a different way and at his or her own speed. Some go back and forth between reading levels and read favorite books again and again. Others read through each level in order. You can help your young reader improve and become more confident by encouraging his or her own interests and abilities. From books your child reads with you to the first books he or she reads alone, there are I Can Read Books for every stage of reading:

SHARED READING
Basic language, word repetition, and whimsical illustrations, ideal for sharing with your emergent reader

BEGINNING READING
Short sentences, familiar words, and simple concepts for children eager to read on their own

READING WITH HELP
Engaging stories, longer sentences, and language play for developing readers

READING ALONE
Complex plots, challenging vocabulary, and high-interest topics for the independent reader

ADVANCED READING
Short paragraphs, chapters, and exciting themes for the perfect bridge to chapter books

I Can Read Books have introduced children to the joy of reading since 1957. Featuring award-winning authors and illustrators and a fabulous cast of beloved characters, I Can Read Books set the standard for beginning readers.

A lifetime of discovery begins with the magical words **"I Can Read!"**

Visit www.icanread.com for information
on enriching your child's reading experience.

I Can Read Book® is a trademark of HarperCollins Publishers.

Walking with Dinosaurs: The Winter Ground
BBC, BBC Earth and Walking with Dinosaurs are trademarks of the British Broadcasting Corporation and are used under license.
Walking with Dinosaurs logo © BBC 2012
BBC logo © BBC 1996
Library of Congress catalog card number: 2013934071
ISBN 978-0-06-223284-7 (trade bdg.)—ISBN 978-0-06-223282-3 (pbk.)
Typography by Rick Farley

13 14 15 16 17 LP/WOR 10 9 8 7 6 5 4 3 2 1
❖
First Edition

I Can Read!

READING
2
WITH HELP

WALKING WITH DINOSAURS
THE 3D MOVIE

The Winter Ground

Adapted by Catherine Hapka

HARPER

An Imprint of HarperCollinsPublishers

Patchi is a young
Pachyrhinosaurus.
He is small but curious.
He and his friend Juniper
were separated from their families.

It happened while the herds
were walking to the Winter Ground.
It was time for the great migration.

But now they are in big trouble!
They can't follow any of the other
dinosaurs that pass by.
Juniper injured her leg.

Now Patchi and Juniper

are lost and alone

in a strange new world.

They stop on a long beach.

The tide is rising fast.

Juniper is too weary to move.

Patchi isn't sure what to do.

A bright red crab darts out
from under a rotting log.
It snaps its pincers.

Patchi is curious.

He has never seen anything

like the crab before!

He moves closer to the crab

and sniffs at it.

SNAP!

The crab's pincers latch
onto Patchi's nose.
Patchi yelps in surprise
and shakes the crab loose.

More crabs appear on the beach.

They surround Patchi

and twirl in a strange dance.

But suddenly a dark shadow

passes over the beach. . . .

13

Patchi looks up.

The shadow of a giant pterosaur

is blocking out the sun.

The pterosaur circles and lands.

It gulps down one crab after another.

Patchi is nervous.

Will the pterosaur eat him next?

He wakes Juniper.

The two of them run up the hill

and hide in the trees.

The forest is dark and spooky.

Night is falling fast.

Juniper's leg is a little better,

but Patchi still must walk slowly

so she can keep up.

Strange sounds and dark shadows
are all around them.
Patchi hears something
rustling in the darkness.

There's another rustle nearby.

Then something bursts into view.

It's only a tiny Alphadon!

Patchi is relieved.

He steps over a tree root.

The root moves!

Juniper's eyes widen in fear.

Patchi just stepped over the tail

of a sleeping Gorgosaurus!

The Gorgosaurus

is a deadly predator.

When he snores, Patchi can see

his huge, sharp teeth.

Patchi tiptoes carefully around
the sleeping giant's curved claws.
Then he and Juniper scamper away
as quickly as they can.

Patchi and Juniper move fast.

They want to get far away

from the sleeping Gorgosaurus.

At first they don't notice

the orange eyes watching them.

More and more orange eyes appear

all around the young friends.

Finally Patchi senses

that they are being watched.

A group of Chirostenotes

appears out of the darkness.

Patchi and Juniper have never seen

such strange-looking creatures!

The Chirostenotes come closer.

At first they seem curious.

Then they start herding

the young friends along with them!

Finally Patchi has had enough.

He snaps at the strange creatures

and chases them all away.

The Chirostenotes flee,

but then the Gorgosaurus appears.

He is wide awake now,
and hungry!
The Gorgosaurus pounces on the
Chirostenotes while Patchi and
Juniper run the other way.

Soon Patchi and Juniper
are all alone once again.
They start climbing a ridge
and reach the edge
of the forest.

A strange greenish light appears beyond the treetops.

The young friends are curious.

They climb as high as they can.

They are at the top of the ridge.

They stare in awe.

The aurora borealis fills the sky.

Dinosaurs fill the valley below.

The two young friends have reached

the Winter Ground!

Patchi and Juniper

rush down the hill.

They find the rest of their herds.

After all their adventures,

they're happy to be back

where they belong.